I Like to Read® books, created by award-winning
picture book artists as well as talented newcomers,
instill confidence and the joy of reading in new readers.

We want to hear every new reader say, "I like to read!"

Visit our website for flash cards, activities, and more about the series:
www.holidayhouse.com/ILiketoRead
#ILTR

This book has been officially leveled by using the
F&P Text Level Gradient™ Leveling System.

# I DIG

## Joe Cepeda

I Like to Read®

**HOLIDAY HOUSE • NEW YORK**

Printed and bound in January 2020 at Tien Wah Press, Johor Bahru, Johor, Malaysia.   •   The artwork was created with Corel Painter and Adobe Workshop.
www.holidayhouse.com   •   First Edition   •   1 3 5 7 9 10 8 6 4 2
This book has been officially leveled by using the F&P Text Level Gradient™ Leveling System.
Library of Congress Cataloging-in-Publication Data   •   Names: Cepeda, Joe, author, illustrator.   •   Title: I dig / Joe Cepeda.
Description: First edition. | New York : Holiday House, [2019] | Series: I like to read | Summary:
"At the beach, a boy digs a tunnel where he finds a crab, starfish, and best of all, a dog"— Provided by publisher.
Identifiers: LCCN 2018006869 | ISBN 9780823439751 (hardcover)   •   Subjects: | CYAC: Excavation—Fiction. | Beaches—Fiction.
Classification: LCC PZ7.C3184 Iaf 2019 | DDC [E]—dc23 LC record available at https://lccn.loc.gov/2018006869
ISBN: 978-0-8234-3974-4 (paperback)

For Lou Henry Whittier Elementary School,
Whittier, California

# Look!

Look!

Look!

I dig.

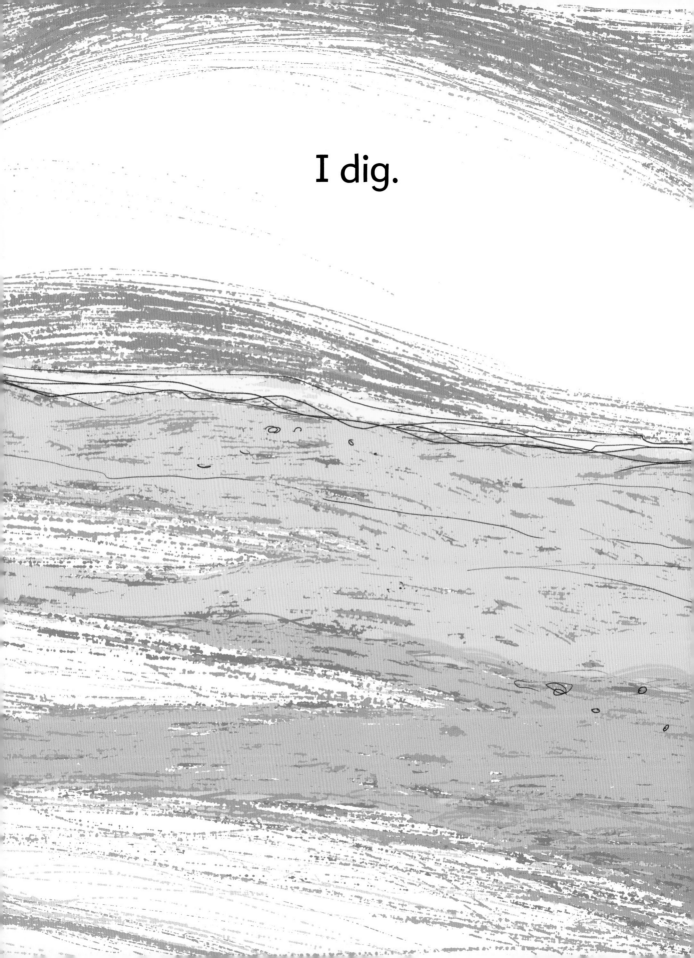

I see a crab.

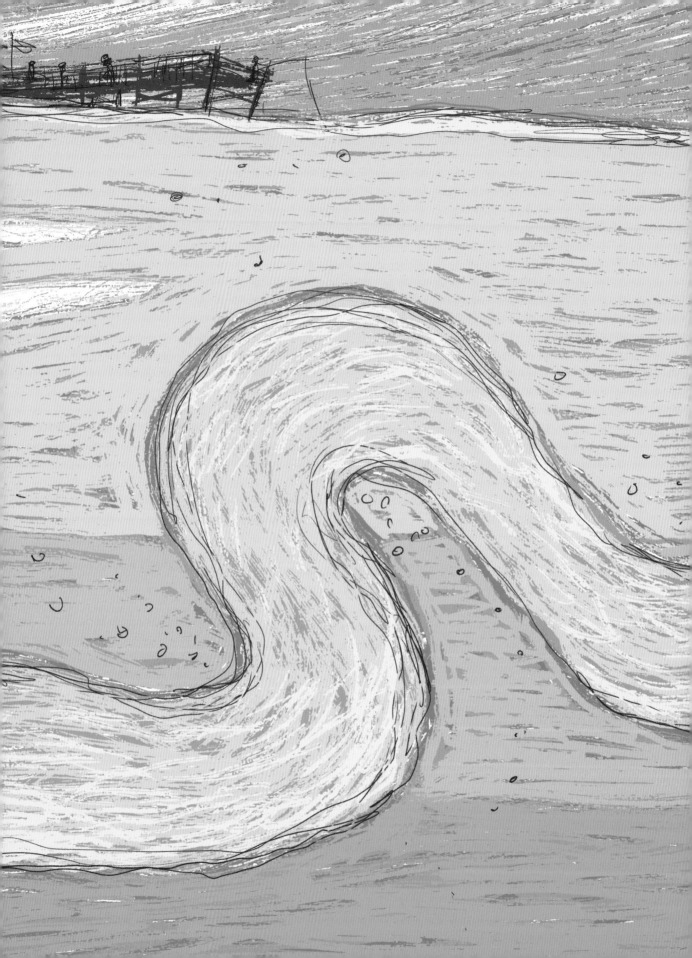

I see stars.

I see a dog.

I go.

I go up.

He is up.

I lie down.

I see stars.

Look!

ALSO BY Joe Cepeda

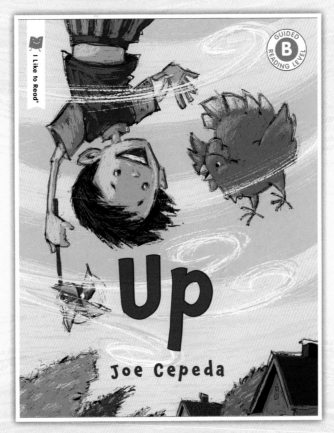